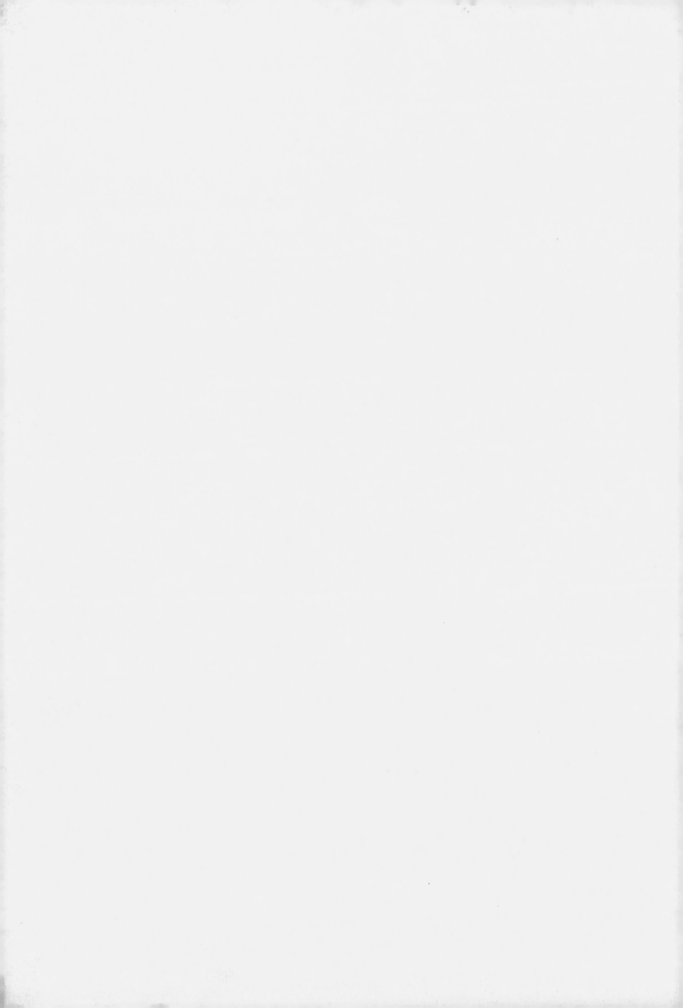

Disney
FROZEN

SPRING FEVER

DISNEY PRESS
Los Angeles • New York

For information address Disney Press, 1101 Flower Street, Glendale, California 91201.

Printed in the United States of America

First Edition, April 2015

1 3 5 7 9 10 8 6 4 2

Target Edition: ISBN 978-1-4847-3760-6

Disney Parks Edition: ISBN 978-1-4847-4381-2

G942-9090-6-15110

For more Disney Press fun, visit www.disneybooks.com

CONTENTS

THE MIDSUMMER PARADE

It was a beautiful summer day. The breeze was soft, the sun was warm, and birds were singing happily. Elsa and Anna were picking wildflowers in a field not far from town.

"I can't believe it'll be midsummer soon," Anna said, looking around the lush green meadow.

Elsa grinned. "I love midsummer," she said. "Remember when we were kids and I used to lead—"

"The midsummer parade!" Anna interrupted, finishing her sister's sentence. The midsummer parade was one of her happiest childhood memories.

"I *loved* that parade," Anna told her sister. "You always looked so fancy, riding at the head of it."

"On that fat little pony," Elsa said with a chuckle. "Mister Waffles."

"We haven't had a midsummer parade since we were little kids," Anna said sadly.

Elsa nodded. "Now that the gates are open, we should have it again. Starting this year!"

Anna clapped her hands. "You'll look so great at the head of the parade," she told her sister.

Elsa grinned slyly. "Not me. *You!* I hereby declare you Midsummer Princess."

Anna, Elsa, and their friends started planning the parade the very next day.

"Marching band?" Elsa said.

"Already rehearsing," Kristoff said.

"Flowers?" Anna asked.

"I've been collecting them all—*achooo!*—week!" Olaf said, sniffling.

Anna consulted the parade planning checklist. "Next up, clothing!"

Anna and Elsa went to search the royal wardrobe.

"How about this?" Anna asked, putting a silly hat on Elsa.

Elsa giggled and held up some boots. "These are definitely you," she told Anna.

The sisters picked wilder and wilder outfits for each other. Soon they were laughing so hard they could hardly stand.

"Okay, it's time to get serious," Elsa said. "You need something special to wear to the parade!"

With a little help from Anna's friends, the parade was shaping up beautifully. It was going to be exactly like when Anna and Elsa were kids! Well . . . almost exactly.

"I don't think you can ride Mister Waffles in the parade," Elsa told Anna. "You're bigger than he is now. Besides, I'm pretty sure he's retired."

"Then I'll have to find a new horse!" Anna said. "The best horse in all of Arendelle."

Anna and Olaf headed to the royal stable to find the right horse. Anna thought the first horse looked very promising . . . until he tried to eat Olaf's nose!

"Hey!" Olaf giggled. "That tickles!"

"Hmmm. What about that one?" Anna asked the head groom, pointing at an elegant mare.

"She's so pretty!" Olaf sighed admiringly.

"This is Lady Crystalbrook Shinytoes the Fourth," the head groom said.

Lady Crystalbrook Shinytoes the Fourth stepped toward Anna . . . and tripped over her own feet. She fell right into the pond!

"Oh, dear," Anna said.

"Oooh. How about him?" Olaf asked, pointing at a big, strong horse. "What's his name?"

The groom cleared his throat. "This," he said proudly, "is Dauntless."

"Hello, Dauntless," Anna said sweetly. As she stepped forward to pet the horse, a leaf fluttered by in the wind. When Dauntless saw the leaf, his eyes widened. With a loud, frightened whinny, he turned and ran away as fast as he could.

"I do *not* think you should ride *him*," Olaf said.

Hours later, Anna was at her wit's end. They had met *every* horse, but they hadn't found the right one. "I don't know what to do," she said miserably. "Maybe we should just cancel the parade."

"Cancel the parade?"

Anna and Olaf looked up to find Kristoff entering the stable. "Why would you do that?" he asked.

"I can't find the right horse to lead the parade," Anna said.

"Hmmm," Kristoff said. "I think I know just the fellow for the job."

"You do?" Olaf said. "Who's the horse?"

"Well . . ." Kristoff said, "he isn't exactly a *horse*."

"Sven," Kristoff said, slinging his arm around the reindeer's shoulders, "how would you like to lead the parade?"

"Gee whiz," Kristoff said in Sven's voice, speaking for his friend, "I'd be delighted!" And Sven *did* look delighted.

"Oh," Anna said, clasping her hands happily, "Sven is *perfect*! He's loyal, and brave, and smart!"

"And handsome," Kristoff added in his Sven voice.

"And handsome," Anna agreed. She kissed Sven's nose.

Anna introduced Sven to the royal stables' grooms. "He's
going to be leading the parade with me," she explained. "So he
needs to look extra fancy."

"It's an honor," the head groom said, bowing low. "Please
come with us, sir."

The grooms set to work on Sven. They oiled his hooves.
They polished his antlers. And they brushed and brushed and
brushed his fur.

When the royal grooms were done with Sven, he positively shone!

"Sven," Anna said, "you look Svendid!" She elbowed Elsa. "Get it? *Sven*did?"

"I get it," Elsa said with a smile. "You really do look magnificent, Sven." Then she frowned. "But I think there's something missing."

Elsa hung a huge flower wreath around Sven's neck.

"There," she said. "Now you're perfect."

Anna looked at the checklist. "Band, flowers, Sven . . . I think everything's ready," she said.

Olaf jumped up and down in excitement. "It's parade time!" he cried.

The birds sang, the band played, and the people of Arendelle cheered as the parade wound its way through town. Anna was so happy she couldn't stop smiling.

The midsummer parade was perfect.

Later Anna and Elsa celebrated the successful parade. "We did it, Anna!" Elsa said. "The parade was just like when we were kids!"

"No," Anna said, grinning at her sister. "It was even better."

THE FROZEN MONSTER

It was a beautiful spring day in Arendelle. Queen Elsa was taking a break from her usual duties to spend time with her sister, Anna.

"Watch out!" Anna cried, speeding through the castle gates on her bike. The townspeople quickly jumped out of her way.

"That's not fair, Anna!" Elsa cried, racing after her sister. "You started before Olaf got to three!"

"First one to the harbor wins!" Anna yelled.

Behind the sisters, Olaf the snowman ran to catch up. "Wait for me!" he said. "Oooh . . . butterfly!"

Anna was almost to the harbor when a huge pile of snow appeared in front of her. She swerved to avoid it as Elsa rode past her, laughing.

"Elsa, using your powers is cheating!" Anna yelled.

"You're just jealous that I'm going to win!" Elsa called over her shoulder.

Just then, Elsa noticed Kristoff and Sven passing in front of her. They looked upset. She quickly stopped her bike to see what was wrong.

Anna raced past Sven, Kristoff, and Elsa. "Ha! Winner!" she called, hopping off her bike. Then she saw her friends' faces, and her smile disappeared. "Kristoff, are you okay?" she asked.

"We've been looking for you," Kristoff said. "Sven and I were gathering ice high in the mountains when we saw something huge in the forest! We tried to get a closer look, but the snow was blowing too hard, and we lost it. Elsa, can you control the snow so we can keep looking for it?"

"You have no idea what it was?" Elsa asked Kristoff.

"It looked like a monster, but I didn't get a good look at it. I thought I knew everything about those mountains, but I guess they can still surprise me!" Kristoff said.

"A new creature? Sounds like an adventure!" Anna said. "Oh! Can I name it?"

"Well, we'll have to find it first," Kristoff said.

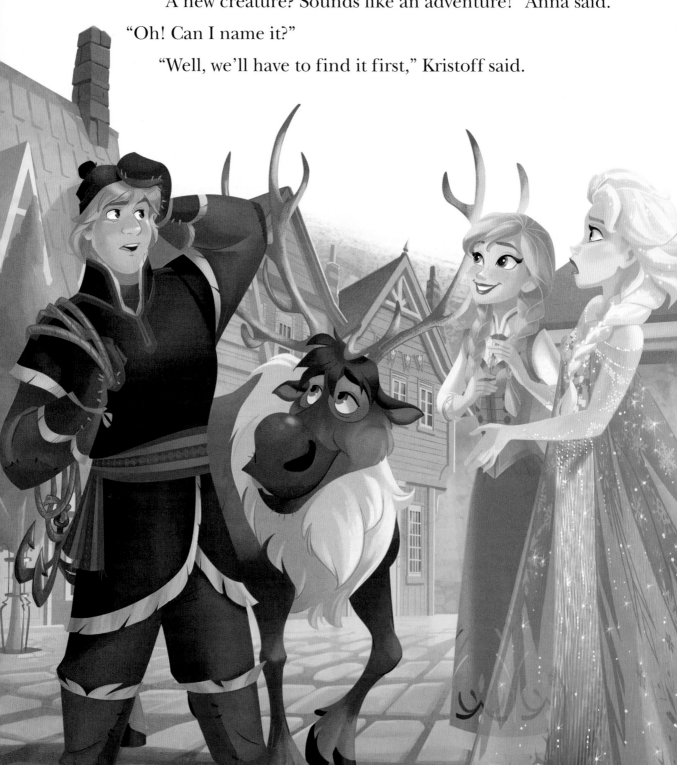

The sisters hurried to the castle for supplies. On their way back to Kristoff and Sven, they ran into Olaf.

"Where'd you go?" the snowman asked. "I was right behind you, and then there was this butterfly, and . . ." Olaf looked at Anna's cloak. "What'd I miss?"

"We're going monster hunting!" Anna said.

"Oooh!" Olaf said. "Can I come?"

With Olaf in tow, the friends set out to find Sven and Kristoff's monster. The higher they climbed, the colder it became. Before long it began to snow . . . hard.

"Hey!" Olaf said, pointing at the snow falling on Elsa. "Now you have a snow cloud, too!"

Olaf happily grabbed Elsa's hands and began to dance with her. Elsa laughed and spun the little snowman around.

"Er, Elsa? A little help here?" Anna said.

Elsa turned to see her sister, Kristoff, and Sven freezing beneath a pile of snow. She quickly parted the storm to clear a path for her friends.

"Whew, that's better," Anna said, brushing herself off. "Now if only we could find our mysterious friend that easily."

"We've been walking for a long time," Elsa said a while later. "Are we almost to where you saw the monster, Kristoff?"

Kristoff and Sven looked at each other. "We . . . ahh . . . don't remember," Kristoff admitted.

"Don't remember!" the sisters said in unison.

"There was a lot of snow," Kristoff said, "and Sven took a wrong turn."

Sven groaned and nodded in agreement.

"How are we going to find the monster?" Anna asked.

Suddenly, a loud roar shook the mountain. Everyone froze.
"Wow, Sven. You sound hungry," Olaf said.
"I don't think that was Sven's stomach, Olaf. I think it was
the monster! Quick! Follow that roar!"
Anna cried.

The group started toward the noise. They hadn't gone far when they heard another roar coming from the opposite direction!

"Are there two of them?" Anna asked.

Elsa stopped and listened. "I think the roar is echoing off the rocks!" she said.

"So how do we find the monster?" Kristoff asked.

Elsa had an idea. She stomped her foot on the snow, and an icy staircase began to grow into the sky. Soon the stairs reached high above the trees. Now they would be able to see the whole forest!

"I never get tired of that," Kristoff said, admiring Elsa's icy creation.

Anna, Elsa, Kristoff, and Olaf began to climb the stairs. Below them, Sven whined. The steps were too slippery for him.

"I'll stay with you, Sven," Olaf said. "Besides, I think I'm afraid of heights!"

As Anna, Elsa, and Kristoff reached the top of the stairs, there was another great roar. "Look! The trees moved over there!" Anna pointed. "That must be where the monster is."

"You mean that patch of trees right next to us?" Kristoff asked.

"Yep!" Anna said.

Kristoff nodded. "Just checking."

At that moment, the trees moved again. The staircase shook.
Sven ran behind the nearest tree, but Olaf had gotten distracted.

"Hello!" he said to a passing bird.

"Olaf, look out!"Anna cried. But it was too late. The
mysterious monster crashed through the trees and stopped right
in front of the snowman.

Olaf looked up. "It's Marshmallow!" he cried.

"Oh, right. Marshmallow! The giant ice monster who tried to attack us!" Kristoff said. "Shouldn't we be running right about now?"

Olaf gave Marshmallow a hug. "Marshmallow isn't scary! He's my friend!" Olaf looked up at the icy monster again. "How's my little buddy?" he cooed.

"He's right, Kristoff," Anna said as she started down the stairs. "Marshmallow doesn't look very scary anymore."

Marshmallow growled sadly. He sank to the ground and hugged Olaf closer.

"Wow, you're a really great hugger," Olaf said. "I think I'm being crushed."

Anna looked at Sven and Kristoff. Then she looked down at her hand, clasped tightly in her sister's.

"I think Marshmallow is lonely," Anna said.

Marshmallow nodded in agreement.

"I'm sorry, Marshmallow," Elsa said. "I thought you would be happy in the mountains. I guess I was wrong. I wish there was something we could do."

Sven and Kristoff looked at each other. They had an idea.

A few days later, Anna and Elsa were in the middle of a rematch race when they spotted a giant figure near the harbor. It was Marshmallow. He was helping Sven and Kristoff deliver ice!

"How's it going?" Anna asked Kristoff.

"Great! Just look how much more ice we've been able to bring down the mountain!" Kristoff said.

Elsa smiled. "Marshmallow seems happy, too!"

Marshmallow nodded as he rubbed Sven's and Kristoff's heads. He was glad to be part of the team!

A Royal Sleepover

"Pssssst! Elsa?" Anna gently nudged her sister. "Wake up."

Elsa shifted, groggy. "Go to bed, Anna," she said.

"I can't sleep!" Anna flopped down on Elsa's bed. Then she smiled slyly. "Wanna have a sleepover?"

Elsa opened her eyes and grinned. That sounded like fun!

Anna went to her room to find extra pillows and blankets.
Meanwhile, Elsa headed to the kitchen to get the ingredients for
her famous honey cones. After all, a sleepover wasn't a sleepover
without snacks!

When Elsa got back to her room, she found Anna digging through the closet. "Aha!" Anna cried. "I knew it was here!"

Anna held up an old, worn book. Her parents had read it to the sisters every night when they were little.

"Let's see, we've got books, games, and this face cream Oaken gave me the last time I went to the trading post," Anna said. She opened the cream. "It looks kinda . . . goopy."

Elsa laughed. "Let's save *that* for later!"

Elsa looked around. It had been a long time since she'd had a sleepover. "Sooo . . . what should we do first?" she asked.

Anna was ready. "How about we build a fort, like when we were kids?" she suggested.

Anna stacked pillows and blankets around the room, making lookouts and hidden caves. Meanwhile, Elsa created icy tunnels and snowy turrets.

"This is fun," Elsa said, putting the finishing touches on an icy archway. "I think we should add a—"

SMACK! Elsa felt something soft and feathery hit her back. She turned to see a fallen pillow and a giggling Anna.

"Oh, no you don't!" Elsa yelled, launching a snowball at her sister. Anna ducked, squealing in delight.

Before long, the room was covered in snow flurries and feathers. Anna was zooming down an icy slide on the fort when there was a knock at the door.

"Is it daytime already?" a familiar voice asked.

"Olaf!" Anna cried. The sisters welcomed their snowman friend inside. Elsa explained that they were having a sleepover and invited Olaf to join them.

"A sleepover?" Olaf asked, excited. "Oh, I've always wanted to have one of those." He paused. "What's a sleepover?"

"We'll show you," Anna said. "Come on! We were just about to play a game!"

Soon the friends were happily playing. Olaf was a natural at Pick-Up Sticks.

And Anna was great at Work of Art. She guessed every drawing and sculpture!

Charades proved to be a bit more challenging. Olaf twisted his body this way and that, making frantic gestures and grinning widely. The sisters didn't know what the answer could be. Finally, Elsa had an idea.

"Olaf, are you acting out 'summer'?" she asked.

"Yes!" he cried. "You're good at this!"

Elsa laughed. "Maybe it's time to do something else," she said. "How about a scary story?"

Anna went first, using her spookiest, most dramatic voice. "According to legend, the Hairy Hooligan only comes out on nights like these, looking for his next victim."

"How do you know when the Hairy Hooligan is around?" Olaf asked.

"He lets out a low moan," Anna answered.

"*OOOOOOOHHHHH.*" A sad whine echoed through the room.

"Wow. That's really scary, Anna," Olaf said, impressed.

"Uh . . ." Anna blinked. "That wasn't me."

"*OOOOOOOOOOHHHHHH!*" The cry sounded like it was coming from outside the castle.

Elsa, Anna, and Olaf ran to the window. There was a shadowy figure walking toward them!

"Stay here," Elsa said, running down the hall. But Anna and Olaf followed. They couldn't let Elsa face the Hairy Hooligan alone!

Elsa opened the castle door, and the friends peered into the darkness. Olaf held Anna's hand, bracing himself for the Hairy Hooligan's pointed teeth and sharp claws.

But it wasn't a monster after all. It was Sven!

"Sven!" Elsa called out. "What's wrong?"

Anna took one look at the reindeer and guessed what was going on. "You couldn't sleep, could you, Sven?" She patted him on the nose. "I bet Kristoff is snoring and keeping you awake. The trolls said his snores are loud enough to start an avalanche!"

Sven nodded.

"You should come to our sleepover!" Olaf said. "From what I can tell, there's very little sleeping involved."

Soon the group was happily settled in Elsa's room.

"How about another story?" Elsa suggested. She held up the book her parents had read to her and Anna all those years earlier.

"Excellent!" Anna agreed. She fluffed some pillows, and she, Olaf, and Sven got comfortable as Elsa began reading.

"'Once upon a time . . .'"

A little while later, Elsa reached her favorite part of the story.

"'And then the brave queen slayed the dragon,'" she read. Elsa stopped, hearing the sounds of heavy breathing around her. The rest of the slumber party had fallen asleep!

Smiling, Elsa put down the book. She gently tucked in Anna, Olaf, and Sven and climbed into bed.

Then, with one last look at Anna and her friends, Elsa, too, drifted off to sleep.

THE ICE GAMES

It was winter in Arendelle—the happiest winter in many years.

Princess Anna and Kristoff were inside, reading quietly in front of a roaring fire. Suddenly, the sound of children's laughter came through the open window. Anna put her book down and went to the window.

"Oh!" she said. "Come look, Kristoff. It's soooo cute!"

Kristoff joined Anna at the window. Three children were building a toboggan in the snowy courtyard below. Kristoff smiled at the children, but Anna could see that he was thinking about something else.

"All right," Anna said. "Out with it. What's on your mind?"

Kristoff turned to Anna. "I didn't have a lot of friends when I was a kid," he said. "I mean, I had Sven. And the trolls. But only humans are allowed to enter the Ice Games."

"The what?" Anna asked.

"Every year on the winter solstice, ice harvesters and their families from all over the world gather on a glacier and hold the Ice Games. It's supposed to be really fun. But you have to have a three-person team." Kristoff looked a little sad. "I bet those kids are building that toboggan for the big race. . . ."

Later Anna told Elsa what Kristoff had said. "It was so sad to hear him talk about missing the Ice Games," she said. "So I was thinking—"

"That we should take Kristoff to the games this year!" Elsa finished for her, delighted. "The three of us can be a team!"

"Yes!" Anna said, hugging her sister. "I knew you'd get it!"

Anna and Elsa quickly packed everything they would need
for the journey to the games. Then they ran to tell Kristoff about
their plan.

"You'd do that for me?" he asked, his face red.

"Of course!" Anna said cheerfully. "Every ice harvester
should get to go to the Ice Games!"

The day before the winter solstice, Anna, Elsa, and Kristoff arrived at the Ice Games. Anna couldn't help staring at the group around her. She'd never seen so many ice harvesters in one place!

"Say," one of them said, pointing at Elsa, "isn't that the queen of Arendelle? I heard she has magic ice powers."

"No fair!" said another. "She'll use her powers to win the games!"

"I promise on my honor as queen that I will not use my powers in the games," Elsa said solemnly.

"Yeah, so back off," said a gruff voice. Anna turned to see a group of ice harvesters from Arendelle standing behind her. With them were the three children she had seen outside the palace window! Anna grinned. She loved that the people of Arendelle were so loyal to her sister.

"Our queen wouldn't cheat," the little girl from Arendelle said. "And she doesn't need to, anyhow."

It was true: Elsa didn't need to use her powers to win the first contest. She carved a gorgeous ice statue of the rock trolls using just a hammer and a chisel.

Next was Anna and Kristoff's event.

"I don't care what the event is. I know we're going to win!" Anna said.

"Couples ice-skating," the announcer boomed.

"Unless it's that . . ." Anna said, her heart sinking. She was a terrible ice-skater.

But Anna wasn't one to back down from a challenge. She and Kristoff gave it their all, swooping and speeding around the rink. Kristoff managed a little jump, and Anna only fell down nine times. They didn't win, but they had a lot of fun trying . . . and they did manage to come in third place.

That night Anna, Elsa, and Kristoff had dinner with the rest of the ice harvesters. As they ate, they discussed the Ice Games.

"With Elsa's first-place finish, and Kristoff and me coming in third in the ice-skating," Anna said, "we actually stand a chance of winning the Ice Games!"

"All we have to do is win the big toboggan race tomorrow," Kristoff agreed.

"Good luck!" Anna heard a small voice behind her say. She turned around to see the little girl from Arendelle.

"Thank you," Anna replied with a smile. "You made the ice sculpture of the palace today, right?"

The girl nodded, blushing furiously.

"It was beautiful," Elsa said. "And I know a little something about making ice palaces!"

Grinning from ear to ear, the little girl ran back to sit with her family.

"Good luck to you, too!" Anna called after her.

"What a sweet little girl," Elsa said. "She reminds me of someone else at her age."

"Me?" Anna asked hopefully.

"I said 'sweet,' Anna. Not 'annoying,'" Elsa replied with a wink.

Anna punched her sister playfully.

"Of course, I meant you, Anna," Elsa admitted.

"One more round of hot chocolate?" Kristoff suggested.

"Yes, please!" Anna and Elsa said together.

As the sun rose the next morning, Anna,
Elsa, and Kristoff piled into their toboggan.
It was time for the last event.

"Here we gooooooo!" Anna shrieked.
The trio rocketed down the slope with
the rest of the racers.

Anna squinted against the
wind as their toboggan went
faster and faster. Soon they
had pulled ahead of the
other racers. "We're
winning!" she
yelled.

Anna, Elsa, and Kristoff were almost to the finish line
when another toboggan passed them. It was moving so fast they
couldn't even see who was inside.

The toboggan streaked down the slope and across the finish
line. It was the children from Arendelle!

"We won! We won!" the kids yelled, hugging each other and
jumping up and down. Watching them celebrate, Anna couldn't
bring herself to be disappointed that she, Kristoff, and Elsa
hadn't won.

She just hoped Kristoff wasn't too upset.

"I'm sorry we didn't come in first, Kristoff," Elsa said later, as they took their place on the winners' podium.

Kristoff grinned. "Nah," he said. "Don't be. I finally got to compete in the Ice Games! And I think it's great that they won. Having friends you can count on is really important when you're a kid."

Anna hugged Kristoff. "Having friends you can count on is really important forever. And I have the best friends of all!"